Rebecca's Ducks

by Angela Moore
illustrated by Nancy Keating

Tuckamore Books
a Creative Publishers imprint

St. John's, Newfoundland
2007

We gratefully acknowledge the financial support of the Canada Council for the Arts,
the Government of Canada through the Book Publishing Industry Development Program (BPIDP),
and the Government of Newfoundland and Labrador through the Department of Tourism, Culture and
Recreation for our publishing program.

Illustrations and book design © 2007, Nancy Keating

Printed on acid-free paper

Published by
TUCKAMORE BOOKS
an imprint of CREATIVE BOOK PUBLISHING
a Transcontinental Inc. associated company
P.O. Box 1815, Station C
St. John's, Newfoundland and Labrador A1C 5P9

Layout by Joanne Snook-Hann
Printed in Canada by:
Transcontinental Inc.

Library and Archives Canada Cataloguing in Publication

Moore, Angela

    Rebecca's ducks / Angela Moore.

ISBN 1-897174-00-4

    1. Picture books for children. I. Title.

PS8626.O5933R42 2006   jC813'.6   C2006-905511-4

Rebecca lived in the big, bustling city of Toronto. She was seven years old and loved many things. She loved vegetable lasagna, the color purple, and her favorite doll, Corinne. But Rebecca was crazy about ducks. She had ducks on her clothes and ducks on her bedroom walls; she sang songs about ducks and read books about ducks. She would have loved to own real live ducks, but she was not allowed. Her family lived in an apartment building where they could not have pets.

Fortunately, there was a park nearby with a little pond full of ducks that she could visit. Rebecca's mom and dad would take her there every weekend so that she could look at the ducks and feed them their favorite food, which was lettuce. She had given them names like Blackspot, Specky, Whitey and Louie.

One day, however, everything changed. Her dad came home from work early with very exciting news. He had found a new job on an oil rig with Hibernia. This meant they could move "back home" to Newfoundland.

Rebecca did not know what an oil rig or Hibernia was, but she had heard of Newfoundland. It was where Nanny Hazel and Poppy Ed lived. Her parents had spoken often about how great it would be if they could go back there, but Rebecca had never been to Newfoundland and did not know if she would like it. She knew she would not like leaving the city and her duck friends behind. This made her very sad.

Two weeks later they loaded everything they owned into the car and trailer, said goodbye to their friends, and headed for their new home. It was a long drive from Toronto, Ontario, to North Sydney, Nova Scotia, where they would catch the ferry to Newfoundland.

It was nighttime when they reached North Sydney, so Rebecca was able to sleep the whole way across on the ferry. In the morning, her dad woke her up and took her out on deck to see the sights. The first thing she saw was water, stretching as far as the eye could see. Rebecca gasped.

"Oh, daddy!" she exclaimed. "That has got to be the biggest pond in the whole world!"

Her dad laughed. "No, honey, that's not a pond. That's an ocean, the Atlantic Ocean, and over there is Port-aux-Basques, Newfoundland."

"Is that our new home?" she asked.

"No, it will be another day's drive before we get there," he told her. "We have to cross all the way to the other end of the island, to the Avalon Peninsula. That's where we'll be living."

When they left the ferry, they drove past great, towering mountains, huge farmlands, rocky barrens, and through lots of wooded areas. By the time they finally reached the Avalon Peninsula, everyone was exhausted.

"We're almost there," said her dad. "We'll be living in a little town in Conception Bay North called South River. For now, though, we'll be staying the night at your Nan and Pop's place."

Rebecca was too tired to get excited about seeing her grandparents. When they finally reached Nan and Pop's house, her dad had to pick her up in his arms and carry her inside.

In the morning, Rebecca was up bright and early, ready to see her family's new home. After a breakfast of Nan's specialty, scrambled eggs with cheese, Rebecca and her parents piled into the car and headed out.

When they pulled into the driveway, they saw a friendly white house with green shutters and a big, red barn in back. Surrounding it all were fields of grass and a cluster of trees. Rebecca was amazed.

"It's like a farm!" she exclaimed. "Oh daddy, this is even better than the city! Are there ducks here, and a duck pond, like at the park?"

"There's a pond right through those trees!" her dad replied.

Rebecca was off and running before anyone could stop her.

"Don't go too far!" shouted her mom.

Through the trees, Rebecca found what she was looking for: the duck pond. The water sparkled a dark blue in the sunlight, and she could hear the sound of a little brook gurgling into the pond, but there was something missing. Where were the ducks?

Rebecca ran back to her parents, who were busy unloading the trailer and bringing their things into the house.

"There are no ducks!" Rebecca cried.

"Don't worry," said her dad. "We'll get some!"

After a few days, when they were all settled in, her parents began to buy some animals. They bought a pony for Rebecca to ride; they bought a cow to give them fresh milk every day; and they bought a whole flock of chickens to give them yummy eggs for breakfast.

Rebecca liked all of the animals, especially the pony, which she named Patch because he was brown with a big, white patch on his shoulder. However, she still wanted ducks because her new home did not seem complete without them. Her parents asked around to see if anyone had ducks for sale, but after days of looking, they came up empty-handed. No ducks.

To console Rebecca, her parents took her to the Salmonier Nature Park to visit the animals. They saw beavers, caribou, moose, lynx and many others. Rebecca liked all of the animals, but she really liked the Canada geese with their black heads and necks, and gray-brown bodies. They reminded her of ducks.

Rebecca left the Nature Park more determined than ever to have her own ducks. Each day, she would go down to her little pond and look at the water, imagining a flock of happy ducks swimming there. She wondered how she could make this dream a reality.

One afternoon, she decided to go for a walk. The day was warm and the birds chirped happily as Rebecca skipped down the road. Not far from her home, she discovered a little path. As she was thinking and wondering if she should follow it, she heard a very familiar sound. It was "quack, quack, quack!" Rebecca ran down the path until she came to the edge of a river. There in the water was a big flock of ducks! At last, she had found them.

Rebecca squealed with delight and bounced on her toes. There were so many of them, and they were so colorful! They were like a rainbow on the water. Most were big and brightly colored, while a few were small and dark. She called to them, but the small ones flew away. The big ones, though, were tame and quickly swam up to her, begging to be fed. Rebecca had nothing to give them, until she remembered that her parents had bought a whole lot of lettuce for the cow and the pony. She ran back and got some for her new friends.

Her mom was almost as happy as Rebecca when she heard about the ducks. Her dad was also delighted when Rebecca told him the good news during his first phone call home from his job on the oil rig.

Every day, for many days, Rebecca went back to the river to feed the ducks. Sometimes she would bring grain, but usually she would bring lettuce or cabbage. Eventually, though, Rebecca's thoughts turned back to the pond behind the barn. It was still empty. How was she to fill it? If only there was a way to bring the ducks from the river to the pond.

Suddenly, she had an idea. The ducks liked lettuce. Maybe, if she had enough lettuce she could coax them back to her pond.

It was a good idea, but she needed lots of lettuce and a way to carry it. Fortunately, her parents still had plenty of lettuce, and her little toy wagon was just perfect for carrying it all. Rebecca ran to the house, dragged her battered blue wagon out of the basement and rushed to the barn. The lettuce was in a bin by the door. Rebecca opened the bin, grabbed the heads of lettuce, and piled them into the wagon. Then she went down to the river to bring the ducks home.

They were all there waiting for her. Rebecca started throwing pieces of the lettuce, first into the water and then onto the land. Fourteen ducks and a big, fat goose gobbled up the lettuce and trailed her back home.

They followed her out past the house, past the barn, through the trees, all the way to the pond. When they reached the water, the ducks quacked and the goose honked happily before waddling into their new home.

Rebecca sat in the grass and watched them swim around in her little pond. They seemed content in their new home, as they splashed, played and dived underwater. Rebecca sighed with satisfaction. Now, she finally had what she'd always wanted: a duck pond filled with lots of ducks...

...and one big fat goose to keep them company!